WHAT BOOKS PRESS

AN IMPRINT OF

THE GLASS TABLE

COLLECTIVE

LOS ANGELES

ECHO UNDER STORY

KATHERINE SILVER

WHAT
BOOKS
PRESS

LOS ANGELES

Publisher's Cataloging-In-Publication Data

Names: Silver, Katherine, author.

Title: Echo under story / Katherine Silver.

Description: Los Angeles : What Books Press, [2019]

Identifiers: ISBN 9781532341489

Subjects: LCSH: Adult children--Psychology--Fiction. | Mothers--Death--Psychological aspects--Fiction. | Dwellings--California, Northern--Fiction. | Proust, Marcel, 1871-1922. À la recherche du temps perdu--Fiction. | Villages--California, Northern--Fiction. | LCGFT: Domestic fiction.

Classification: LCC PS3619.I5483 E34 2019 | DDC 813/.6--dc23

Cover art: Gronk, *Untitled*, watercolor and ink, 2018
Book design by Ash Good, www.ashgood.design

What Books Press
363 South Topanga Canyon Boulevard
Topanga, CA 90290

WHATBOOKSPRESS.COM

ECHO UNDER STORY

for L, A, and U, of course

To be again of a sudden
as fragile as a second,
to feel again as deeply
as a child facing god,
that is what I feel right now
at this most fertile instant.

—*Violeta Parra*

Thus he perceives that the real problem, even without God, is the problem of psychological unity . . . and internal peace. He also perceives that this is not possible without discipline that is difficult to reconcile with the world. That is precisely the problem. One must reconcile it with the world.

—*Albert Camus*

(Note: all footnotes are quotes from *A la recherche du temps perdu*, by Marcel Proust, Éditions Gallimard, 1954, in my English version, with thanks to Andrew Wilson.)

act 1

The car is packed with all things needed to spend a few days in a house nearly empty. The road along the way is lined with new green grass, the hillsides are dirt brown, still brown, a darker brown than usual, the dark brown of three years of drought that one stormy night, five nights ago, does not turn to green, but it does bring local relief. A red-tailed hawk with a rabbit, maybe still alive, in its talons, wings along the road. The bay, really a fjord, is bluer than the partially overcast sky, a sliver of the sky from a different day cut out and set down, a pane of textured glass between the forested hills to the west and the rolling brown hills to the east.

Upon arrival she unloads the car and sets up a bed and a rudimentary kitchen. There is work to do and have done, arrangements to be made, projects to evaluate and oversee, options to discuss. Practical purpose is foremost, but the dark part of the day cycle is long and here there is more silence. So: words.

She grew up in this house her parents built. Her mother, whom I'll call E, died in this house five years ago and for five years it has been rented out to strangers. Only once during that time did she drive up the driveway, but she never climbed the stairs and never crossed the threshold. In order to finish setting up the kitchen for her short stay, she has to decide on which shelf in which cupboard on which surface to put the pepper and salt shakers, where the sugar, where the tea, and where the olive oil. She vacillates: maybe the way always done is best, and it would be flailing rebellion to do otherwise; or maybe the old ways are better questioned, and an improved order, or one that better suits, here now in this instant, created.

She knew the journals were here, stashed away behind a small door inside a closet in the back room, but still she feels a stir when touching them. Maybe she hoped the tenants had destroyed them, inadvertently, the way their elusion of the flames throughout E's life may also have been inadvertent. More than twenty notebook volumes, the notebooks themselves of varying sizes and styles, though organizing them by date reveals several stretches when three or four of the same kind were used consecutively. Almost but not all are lined, she notes while leafing before organizing them. Some of the lined pages are narrowly lined, some broadly. The penmanship and ink are also inconsistent. If one didn't know for certain that they were written by the same person, one might harbor doubts.

For long months at a time, even years, the writing is tidy and cramped, each letter perfectly and patiently formed, usually with a narrow nib, sometimes a drafting pen, and some notebooks are entirely filled with thicker lines from broad italic nibs. Suddenly, within one volume, the penmanship abruptly changes, words are treated differently, sometimes even on a single page: here as ends in themselves, lovingly drawn, a boon; there, a necessary evil, a bane, dashed off in a frenzy, with disdain, the sooner dispensed with the better. Then, only initial letters of most words are clearly legible, the rest flatlined, as if her mind were racing ahead of her hand and the word taking shape had already been relegated to history before coming fully into form.

It used to seem that sequence mattered, had consequence, but by now too many stories have been told. Some people repeat the same stories often and at the feeblest of prompts, repeating the stories they live by. The journals, thankfully, are not stories, not even remotely. One could in theory construct a story in hindsight, pick and choose in order to stimulate interest, impose an arc on what was only meant to hold one after another particular moment. The sequence is of the life lived, now over, and only true as contrivance to someone who tells her story over and over, the stories people of a certain age live by.

E read Proust's exploration of time past or lost three times in the last ten years of her life while she was confined to this house. More precisely: she read it twice then died while it was being read to her a third time. In the middle of the fifth volume. Albertine.

In addition to returning to the house and considering what to do with the journals, her daughter is reading Proust and is now nearing the end of the second volume. She read the first two volumes of Proust many years before. Except for parts of *Swann in Love*, or possibly only the title, she recognizes nothing she is reading, as if another moi or I or self had read it, as if her memory had retained, or cognitive faculties absorbed, nothing whatsoever of what she had read. She begins to recognize that at least one of Proust's overriding passions is the search for the sinews that connect the past to the present, the person writing to the person being written about, whether it be his child or adolescent self or Swann's various selves from man-in-love to man married. The narrator veers sharply away from his opening gambit, his memories of childhood in Combray, into realms connected presumably by thin sinews, a sharp turn that includes an abrupt shift in narrative perspective, from the intimate I probing into that younger moi, narrating the sensations, thoughts, conjectures the narrating I would have access to, to a wholly (for moments) omniscient third-person magician who has access not only to the events he could not possibly have witnessed (intimate scenes between Odette and Swann, for example) but also to the consuming experience of love and jealousy, as well as higher-level speculations about the nature of love and desire and loss, for example, making fine, superbly fine distinctions between the loss of the object of one's love and the loss of the experience itself of love.

❖ ❖ ❖

They shouldn't be stashed back away, not yet. Damp and bugs and decay will finally make all of them illegible. To discard or simply ignore them is a shame, if only because the ink shows a wide range of color and density. Do the lines drawn, the letters shaped, penetrate the page, or does the paper maintain its integrity behind the ink? How dark or daring is that ink? There are green tones and less often blue, these besides black, which prevail. All this gleaned from a quick glance through the pages. *Here, with you, I can be alone, I can hear my own thoughts*, she wrote, addressing those pages, that ink.

Context—we say and repeat and this has even become a dogma—is everything. And yet these journals can be read only out of context. They exist out of context, out of that cubbyhole behind the wall inside the closet, out of the places and people they record erratically, the perceptions and emotions those people and places evoked. The words are drawn on pages in notebooks bought somewhere, carried somehow, opened by someone, and that person, now gone, those contexts, now vanished, only the words now remain, with dates (this is true). The question that occurs to her on this second day in this house after spending several hours ripping up an invasive vine that had grown into the shed under the deck and pushed through the siding, all but staunching the two white rose bushes she planted after E's death, five years from today, is whether context can be said not to matter? If it is possible to conceive of a text, even a sentence, without context. Language itself contextualizes, language as the commons, employed in a particular time and place after and before another time. And already extensively used. The names of the roses are Madame Alfred Carrière and Souvenir de la Malmaison. The strenuous growth of the Madame Alfred Carrière pushes through the makeshift fencing, and the deer eat what they can reach. The Souvenir de la Malmaison, somewhat stymied, has less to offer. She opens the fencing and removes the thinnest and most scraggly branches, jumbled and sickly shoots, then closes it as best she can.

The rain has continued. The hills are tingeing green. Mulch is happening. On this second drive across the bridge to the house a rainbow is making landfall over the state penitentiary. How could that be? Why should that not be? More rot than cracks are showing. The deck must go, all of it, top to bottom, and then be rebuilt. There are holes in the box around the electric meter where mice have eaten through the board-and-bat redwood siding. The siding on the south-facing wall is burned, charcoaled by fifty years of direct yearlong sun, and warped, offering further opportunities for rodents to enter the walls and therein make homes for themselves. The linoleum floors in the three bedrooms have been ripped up along with the underlying particle board; exposed are pine planks with large knotholes and gaps in between, then empty space between them and the ground. Rats could get in there. She reconsiders sleeping on a mattress on the floor in the main room, then rolls up towels and shoves them under the doors to the bedrooms. The fire is burning on slow, and the ceiling fan circulates the warm air quietly.

Con text. With words. A joining together, a weaving, of the woven textured cloth.

❖ ❖ ❖

Closer inspection reveals that many of the journals are, indeed, unlined. First impression: that she felt compelled to write them to capture life as it was being lived. The passing of so many perceptions without a trace bothered her and these books were a hedge . . . *the total absurdity of it all, how stupid of me to try to understand anything. Yet that, too, is too easy an out, too comfortable an excuse . . . For, after all, though it might be beyond us, we still must try to grasp what we can. If asked why I bother, I must say, "Each animal uses the faculties it has to survive, and reflection is mine."* Traces left in pages. Against oblivion? She smiles at futility, in this and so much else, she conjures the unimaginable mass, hence gravity, of all perceptions had by all people of all nations since time immemorial. Could there be a storage site? But maybe E was trying to do something more circumscribed, and immediate. To discover this, she knows she will have to methodically read through the journals. She thinks this is the least she can do, regardless of futility. I think it is the most and an attempt worthwhile.

Her eyelids are leaden. The bed beckons. The fire has almost burned itself out. Rain has started to fall. At first it is an edging out of silence. Then a rush. Not drops. Not discrete sounds at regular intervals. Rather, a splurge of noncount nouns. The rain gutter along the east side of the house is clogged with leaves and other detritus, and water is dripping over its top in the corner where it will run back under the house. She mollifies her urge to rush out in the rain and dark to clear out the drain by telling herself that the water is doing now what it has been doing for three years. But the drought. There is a headlamp, but no rain gear. Tomorrow, she'll set up the ladder and act as if she were convinced that she is here and responsible for all this. This will make it true.

The rose bushes deserve to be free yet protected from the deer. The constant nibbling may have strengthened their roots but it is time they push upward.

She leafs through one notebook. A page here. A paragraph there. Then she picks up another and does the same. She looks for concrete referents, details, to orient her to the little she knows about her mother's life. About the places she lived, more or less in order. About the ships she worked on during the war and after. About the Kamikaze raids and the stoic Norwegians and the volume of Ovid lurched overboard in a storm. About paper money carried in wheelbarrows in Peking; about the hoards of starving in the streets; about how Americans shouted to make the Chinese understand. A picture of her with an American sailor in a booth in a restaurant, swirled with smoke from the cigarette between her fingers near her face (elbow leaning on table). A starving but dashing Russian sailor she danced with and almost married. Greenwich Village in the forties. Bohemia. Gomorrah. Her disapproving Stalinist father. Marriage, children, divorce. She looks, in vain, for signposts, clues as to who or what or where.

She finds E's own reflections on her practice. *But what is really being talked about here?* She flips through the pages, feeling more and more impatient. *The abstract is wonderful but it helps to combine it with elements of the concrete so that two hours later I know where I was and what I was thinking about when I wrote it.*

The deck is rotten, the skylight in the bathroom is leaking, louvers are missing from the window, siding is breaking free, rain gutters and downspouts are clogged, and now, the drain under the kitchen sink is hanging open and loose, and when the water was run a bit harder, it overflowed, flooding the sink cabinet and the floor. There's a drip inside the toilet tank, and the drain in the bathroom also leaks, but only very slightly. If she didn't have moments like this one when she hears only the crackling of the last embers in the fireplace, a ladybug rustling inside the paper lantern above the kitchen table, and the refrigerator, which should be exiled for its muted and stupefying roar, she might conclude that the time and money she is currently spending on the renovations of the house, for the sake of posterity, out of loyalty to legacy, are not worth the effort. But she has these moments. Why does what lies beyond the night-blackened window matter to the rhythm of the heart and the sediment in the mind? Dark curtains can hide a throbbing, fulminating urban landscape teeming with individual humans and all the stuff we make and cherish and keep and throw and use and abuse. She cannot know through her senses what's there on the other side of the glass. She cannot know through her senses that for as far as she could ever walk in a day or many there is mostly unroaded, uninhabited forest and rotting wood and leaf and mushroom mulch and sand and ocean. She cannot know through her senses that there's a sparse sprinkling of humans and that these keep relatively quiet so as to extend as much as possible the persistence of solitude, the spread of untrammeled time, interludes that let the embers be rendered into ash, the crackling grow slow, and to wonder whether sleep will come before the sparks die.

❖ ❖ ❖

In one sentence she is *full of the moment*, in the next, *I am drained, extenuated, debilitated*. She will often use two, more often three, synonymous words or phrases. As if groping for precise meaning. Or an intuitive sense of the rule of threes. The synonyms build on each other, or flatten each other, but this isn't a literary critique. And although she often claims that only in those pages, shielded from the eyes of the world, can she *be herself,* can she *eschew the glance or glare of the world*, there is something else at work. Of course, there must be. The journals were not destroyed.

It's the human that's become so troubling. Both in the abstract and in the sensate, in touch and sight and hearing. For starters: the endless and impenetrable narcissism of species. The petty puffing up of individual egos can be mere preening, but the project of humanity to build a tower and reach the heavens, to crack the code and paint the deity in our image, claiming it was the other way around: could there be greater hubris as a whole? Even one who lives in reclusion cannot escape her own company, in all its humanness, nor avoid carrying the commons of language in the forefront of the mind, sifting all impressions through its screens and winnowing the best into new and pretty combinations. The trick might be in finding the crack, the thoroughfare. Or not having a trick. Turns of phrase. The commons.

Even here, in the silence, especially here, in the silence, she is troubled by the lack of response from local contractors and carpenters. They don't call her back, or if they finally do and come to take a look, she leads them around the property, spends hours explaining to him and then to the other what is needed, and listens to much-appreciated advice. But then she doesn't hear back, or she does and they are busy for the next six months, and she sits in the silence, and she wakes up in the middle of the night—when the silence is deep, save for some rustling, a buck on the hillside behind the house— worrying about the money going out and not coming in, because when it's over she'll have to rent the house out anyway, this house where E lived and died, where the journals lay stashed for decades, now out on a table for her perusal, and where she, now, is spending a few stolen hours of solitude and silence on the edge of the enormous open space, where she will, tomorrow, sit by the bay and look for loons, who are anything but common. Or, as E wrote in one of the notebooks: *How does the conversation you hold constantly with yourself—even when nobody is listening, the conversation is still ongoing—how does it make you feel? Do you need third parties to break it up, liven the mood, change the tone?*

❖   ❖   ❖

Memories, the making thereof, the recording thereof, the storing up of impressions, sometimes on a page, this under a ray of what used to be called optimism, which often accompanies youth, a side dish to strong limbs, optimism that there will be enough future to dispel endings and make words matter. As if in the absence of making memories, not much of which E was doing in her last ten years in her chair in her house above that small valley in that village on that peninsula, almost an island, connected to the mainland along a deep and abiding fault, there, in her chair with her back to the oak trees and the bay forest rising up from the other side of the valley, she read Proust, perhaps (here, a moment of my own speculation) to learn ways to live with and through the memories already made, ways to transform them, summon them, create new combinations out of the old, voluntary and involuntary, but always willing: the scent that arises, the sudden encounter with a crooked cobblestone, the taste of a cookie, the impressions one has when one arrives for the first time in a new place or in a place where one spent most of one's youth but never saw as one is seeing it now.*

The sky is always elsewhere, but today the sky does not respect boundaries. It spills over the line of treetops along the ridge across the valley and pours down the hillside toward her, sliding under the crowns of the bishop pines and caressing the understory of madrones and low-growing manzanitas and salal and huckleberry and coffeeberry and so much else. The coming storm will fell some trees now standing, and the path will be littered with debris from the flowing water and leaves and branches brought down by the weight of water and wind. Even the birds are keeping close to their quarters, or so the hushing says. A few rustles in the underbrush, birds or possibly rabbits, a squirrel. One song of three longer notes and a descending trill, but the singer is nowhere to be seen. A hummingbird whistles, quivers, swooshes by just above the bushes along the path. On her way down, she takes the path that is deliberately though partially hidden near the top where it branches off from the main switchback trail. Just as she thinks it is petering out and the only option will be to retrace steps and rejoin the main trail, the path generously opens. Even then, at several turns, the continuation is hidden, doubts gain weight.

The first time she took this side trail and reached the lower main trail that follows the contour of the mountain rather than climbs, winding, to the top, there was a sense of relief and accomplishment, discovery and excitement, and a hue of uncertainty at ever finding it again. This second time: wistful delight at the end of a reverie. From this side path, the vistas are wider, the eye can wander anywhere through the full expanse of the watershed and not be assaulted by human pockmarks, and the bay, really a fjord, lays down its loosely twisted silk ribbon, today not blue, to separate the forest from the barren hills. The continent there and stretching beyond the senses; this forest, this land, open, pristine, and all its beings, mostly still, to her, unnamed. So it has been, exactly like this as far as the eye can see, her entire life. The deck may be rotten and the plumbing leaky and the insulation negligible, but to be here now is extraordinary, unnamable.

Night is deepening, though still distinct is the faint outline of the ridge of bay laurel trees against a slightly lighter sky. One more sentence and it will be gone and nothing but black beyond the glass. The fire is young and needs tending, not constant tending, but attention. Her past loves parade through the flames, dancing in and out of the flickering and sometimes holding on to the ephemeral tongues that curl off and between the logs, ghost lovers, prancing through other lives than hers and theirs from then. The longing is not for them. The question is if such feelings could ever be roused again, if a living person not a ghost could summon even a shade of what was lived so long ago with those who no longer exist. In one of the journals she skimmed that day, she found: *When we make love we are perfect.*

For someone lacking even the most elementary poetic sensibility, how can a self be constructed? Or is the impulse to construct one a poetic impulse in itself, an impulse unknown to those who disregard the involuntary, the message in the fog? The most salient feature of E's journals, what she has gleaned from her peripatetic reading, is their undying optimism, which E did not exhibit with any consistency in her life, at least in the limited slices of her life that her daughter was in a position to observe. Even at those recurrent moments of adolescent angst, when she says repeatedly that, *All I want to do is crawl away in a hole and die*, writing is an act of obscene but absolute hope, faith, belief, while in her descriptions of the self that she is reflecting upon there is only despair and disgust. The self that writes believes in the next moment, holds up the possibility of meaning, story, a future moment when someone, one of the selves she knows she contains or an imaginary being who will come across her or her journals, will read those words, rendering them worthy of drawing in ink.

Writing is an act of obscene but absolute hope, faith, belief. The self that writes believes that the next moment will hold out the possibility of meaning. Then, this: *What is the particular quirk that gives us sight and vision, sound and hearing, knowledge and thought? And which also sometimes fails me so utterly.*

M wants to leave D. She does not want to hide. I am all discouragement. We would not survive the aftershock.

M sweeps me away. Do I want to go? Where will the dust settle?

M has succumbed. Marriage, status, wealth, class, privilege. D will scorn me. A Jew, a radical, and that's only the beginning.

Love keeps returning. *Is love an entity?* she asks. *How can I be so full of something that doesn't exist apart from me?* A few pages later come frustration, pain, despair, solitude after all, the inability to bridge the gap *between one skin and another no matter how hard or for how long two skins press against each other, into one another, still there is that crack, the one that lets the light in but also leaves us wrapped in our own cocoon.* And each time—for there are several times, as far as can be gleaned because separated by pages, years, and interspersed with despair that is never specific to circumstance—love is monumental and devotional. But never a name. At most, an initial. *G is particularly punishing today. I must avoid the blows or do something to deserve them.*

She avoids gender with dexterity, as if someone were looking over her shoulder.*

---

* *Personally I thought it absolutely irrelevant from a moral point of view whether one found one's pleasure with a man or with a woman, and only too natural and human to look for it wherever one could find it.* (III, 686)

26

She found hedgehog mushrooms on her walk today. It's early for them: the heavy rains and warmer weather. Not enough for a meal, but their color suffices. Does that color have a name? And how can it be just enough different from any other color popping up out of the mulch far beneath the towering bishop pines?

◈　◈　◈

Now, here, in this house, never elsewhere or since her death, memories of E are unlike any other memories she has ever had. *Memory* might not be the right word. Past time or lost time or time discovered, found, found again, or encountered. But never regained. The market is never in play. Memories can be evoked, often by a sensual trigger, then encouraged to peak out, coaxed to emerge then expand, often by an act of will, a self that has something to gain thereby. They include an event, a passage of time, or a sharp, pungent sensation. There is often a story. Here, now, E simply appears, most recently in the shower, sitting on the pull-down bench installed for her after her stroke. The warm water is washing over her body. A large and very strong nurse's aide is soaping her then helping her up and out. The memory, such as it is, does not evoke a particular feeling. Maybe this is what some people call a ghost.

We spend much of our lives trying to distinguish ourselves from our parents: to be whom we imagine we can be, not what we have seen and seen through and are even repulsed by. Somebody is watching but is not acting upon the process of becoming. Or becoming no longer is and simply accommodates itself to being. Healthy in body, this the physical condition, she is in the shower enjoying the strong current of hot water on her head and back and over her breasts and shoulders, and E is also there, enjoying the hot water over her back and shoulders and breasts, and she will be her and she was once her, the spot holds (except for the rotation of Earth) and all times join in a ghostly present of multiple moments of the two of them. Just the two of them, no matter how many we are.*

---

* *Perhaps for a daughter such as Mamma, the great sorrow that follows the death of her mother merely breaks the chrysalis that much sooner, hastens the metamorphosis and the arrival of a being that we carry inside, and that would have arisen more slowly without this crisis, which makes us shoot ahead and leap over phases in a single bound . . . After she is dead, we feel qualms about being different, we admire only what she was, which we already were though mixed with something else, and what we will henceforth exclusively be. It is in this sense . . . that we can say that death is not futile . . . Lastly in this cult of grief for our dead, we vow to worship what they loved . . . even the volumes of Mme de Sévigné that my grandmother carried with her wherever she went . . . (II, 769)*

To return to this house is also to return to this village. The village comprises two valleys, First and Second, and a Mesa in between. She now hears talk of a Third Valley, though this one necessarily remains apart because it cannot be reached from Second as First and Second can be reached from each other over the Mesa out the door of the house and via a trail that passes through a neighbor's property. A two-lane highway runs through the one-block town and continues out to the beaches and parklands and hiking trails of the public lands. At the moment, in the town, which has seen better days and worse days over the years, there is a café where one can sit and have a coffee, at least on weekends. The café is attached to a highbrow restaurant with very few and expensive choices for dinner. Past the post office there is and always has been an Eastern European bar and restaurant. It is forbidden territory, ostensibly because the food is bad, though she suspects the prohibition originally had to do with early- to mid-twentieth century European politics and war. Locals who want to run into other locals for a brief exchange might go to the post office right around noon, soon after the day's mail has been sorted and placed in the boxes. So far, besides the people she knew as a child or has met over the years through E, most of the locals with whom she has interacted are in the building trades. People here like to place each other, find the thread in the web along which each resides, establish the points of juncture and degree of separation. The family names she knows from long ago have exclusive use of her memory and retain therefore a degree of reality and truth that no others are able to attain. Secondary connections also hold the web together and are recognized as such. For example, J, the man she has hired to build a retaining wall and a more solid support in front of the back bedroom window for the wisteria that weighs heavily on a rotting and rickety wood frame, appeared at first to be knowledgeable and trustworthy, but he does not always respond to her phone calls and emails. Many days pass without word about when he will start the project, and whenever she insists, he becomes the one dispensing favors. Rain has been frequent all month but not unabated. It's not a good idea to cut into the slope for a retaining wall when rain threatens, he says with a sharp edge. Two days later another email, this time edgeless. As it turns out, he writes, he plays tennis with P, who referred to her as a good friend, a "dear" friend. She responds by return email that likewise she considers P a dear friend. J's tone has changed. A similar secondary connection is established with M, the man who is rebuilding the deck and will probably do a lot of other jobs around the place, such as ripping out and replacing the front door sill, which has dry rot, replacing the siding on the house facing the deck, and building a new shed under that deck. He makes his suggestions with longwinded and meandering explanations that she understands only very vaguely, and she has learned how to stop listening but keep nodding.

How we divide up landscape, define place, draw borders is much like how we tell ourselves stories and both are affected by our proximity or distance, our adherence to stories we've heard, where we put the salt and pepper, where the plastic bags we'll reuse. We grow up in a mythical landscape and return to find the magic gone but nothing to replace it. "The magic has gone out of our world," though that is a tautology, for to call it magic is to know, even if not to admit, that it is gone, for the animation of other beings was not magic, reality simply included many more and different voices. Our ears were tuned, our eyes perceived differently. What a racket we summoned once we stopped listening.

She first found the journals shortly after E died, while she was packing up and emptying out this house for the tenants. Three days later, after everything had been removed and other family members had left, she stashed the journals back into the wall inside the closet where she knew neither the tenants nor anybody else would ever find them. Then she remained alone with the unfaded squares on the redwood-paneled walls where pictures had hung, the depressions in the rugs where furniture legs had pressed, the tawdry lifeless lackluster of the few things that remained for the tenants: the piano, an old corduroy couch, the dining room table E made many years ago out of a desktop. The bedroom where E died is next to the main room—kitchen, dining room, and living room with a large, brick fireplace. She went in there, crouched down on the old linoleum floor, and wept.

The journals, she reasoned, belonged to the house.

There's a voice that says: Do not betray the trees along the ridge, the birds hopping in the unseen-by-me dawn, the fog rising from the valley, the footprints of the fox or raccoon who found the open car window and placed its muddy paws on every upholstered surface. It says: Do not spoof their truth.

There's also her voice, though more of a tinny echo. Again: a ghost. To re-create a dialogue: contrived. Because the voice we hear is not written down. Sounds something like: What the hell are you doing? Seems to say: I never tore it down, ripped it up, pulled it out, bashed it in. And the gestures nobody can see. She winces; she shakes her head in barely resigned horror. Still there's a chance to answer back, also intoning. The distance between life and death might allow for a civil conversation. But she's dead, she says, cruel as she feels herself whenever she is inclined to heed the words she doesn't actually hear. The option: to let E be alive. To let her think she is alive. To let her keep talking in the background. What the hell are you doing? And so, in response: What the hell did you do all those years? I'm using the money you scrimped and saved on your house, my house, our house, this house, in this village, and by the way, I've been clearing the ivy away from those oak trees. Finally something she'll approve of. A few dying tanoaks and some bay laurel, but the live oaks form an almost perfect halo. E often complained about the trees, how fast they grow and how expensive the tree work is, how difficult it was for her to keep up with it. She's been clearing ivy away from those oak trees, cutting the strangling vines at the bottom. Because the oak trees.

And all along, what she'd like to ask is: Where is the lid of the septic tank? Where is the leach field? Where does the other end of that black pipe drain? They are pulling up the steel t-posts and rusted chicken wire that comprised a deer fence around a small section of the flat space below the house. No gate to speak of, just another piece of chicken wire attached with another wire to a two-by-four to keep it rigid. And the wood pile.

As for plantings, E left only the wisteria, and a *Garrya elliptica*, whose silk tassels she loved, and right now it is tasseling, a triumph of tassels.

There are oak trees lining the lane that leads from the house to the forested hills. She passes them often and notices their moods. The ones around the house as well though she eschews their moods for fear they might interfere with hers. One wishes to maintain boundaries and hold a pious distance from one's neighbors. In collaboration with the neighbor to the east, she places stakes in the ground and stretches a string between. Her land goes past the plum tree and down the small knoll, farther than she'd ever known it to go.

By the ocean. At sunset. The sky sank into the lagoon and the coot dove down and found it.

The trick is to find a language as tender as the fog slipping down the narrow bay, as essential as each blade of grass poking out of the brown earth after the year's first rain, as sharp as a clam's snap, as roiling as the hidden eddy of the incoming tide. To find a language as bleached and pristine as a cow's skull in the sand. That would be something. That would be everything.

She returns the journals to their place without having read them thoroughly. E was, after all, the most private of people, and even if a shadow of desire to be read had lasted as long as her breath, her daughter can no longer summon imaginary impunity for her trespass.

These pages . . . my refuge . . . my lost savior . . . my paradise lost . . . I call you lost for you no longer serve me as you did before . . . abandoned by you, first and foremost, I stand now more alone than ever.

❖ ❖ ❖

act 2

She is not one to presume, particularly not a proximate cause to any emotion that she or anybody else might experience. But she is struck by the seeming of a strong link between the rain and her well-being, the experienced quality of the day's texture. If, for instance, a miracle should happen and all predications modeled and mottled and based on measurements were dead wrong, and at this moment she heard a muffled shushing, a sound like fabric swirling that grew steadily louder until rain was unmistakably falling, the world will have become other, and this world currently inhabited, one she once knew and was glad to turn her back on.

By now, weeks of unraveling. The destruction has peaked and wrecking gives way to erection, order, beauty, utility, the delusion of settling that lasts long enough to fool the most astute among us. At the moment, a welcome touch of that delusion while the recollection of chaos is constructed. The house was tented and fumigated. The interior now feels more solitary, no ladybugs flitting from light source to light source or brushing up against the sides of a lamp shade, the hum of their wing-flutter. Their absence, though sad, offers her finally a sense of belonging to our exterminating species, resigned to collateral damage. More solitude in the face of the abyss between what we are and the stories we construct about ourselves. Mirrors of our own making. Even more shimmering: our gods.

The entire month of January has passed with no rain; to think, as she does, that December was so promising.

E began reading Proust after her initial illness, when her life, reduced to a minimum of novelty, had come firmly under the reign of habit, even to the extent that her reading chair faced into the room, its back to the green wall of forest, mostly bay laurel with other identifiable trees especially along the ridge. Proust is interested in the difference between how we experience the world—perception and lived experience, these two things distinguished by the distance at which we stand—when habit holds sway and when not. Habit, in a sense, becomes a presence, one that accompanies us closely. And about what happens when there are no repetitive motions that blunt our appreciation of the spectacle of reality.*

---

* *It is usually with our beings reduced to a minimum that we live; most of our faculties lie dormant because they rely on habit, which knows what there is to do and doesn't need them. But on this morning of travel, the interruption of my routine existence and the shifting of place and time had made their presence indispensable.* (I, 656)

Tonight she will sleep in E's bedroom rather than on the floor of the main room. The floors in the bedrooms are now maple planks, the deck is still missing the deck boards and railings, and the shed underneath remains unfinished. Most of the terrain surrounding the house is cluttered with piles of lumber and other construction detritus. The house was fumigated, and when the tent was removed, the oldest, most gnarly and sculpted section of the old wisteria broke off, and the root ball, anyway half rotten at the crown, probably right above the original graft onto the rootstock, was upended. She doesn't think it will survive and flower in spring. It might be spring already. There is no rain in the forecast. The green of the hills is turning brown again, and the soil is turning to dust.*

❖　❖　❖

* *Bygone days slowly cover those that preceded them, and these in turn are buried under the ones that follow. But each bygone day is lodged inside us as in an enormous library, where there is one volume among the oldest books that nobody, surely, will ever request. When, after passing through the translucency of the subsequent epochs, that bygone day rises to the surface and spreads out inside us until it covers everything, then names take back their former meanings, beings their former faces, we our spirits of that time, and we feel, with vague sorrow that has become tolerable and will not last, the problems that long ago became unsolvable and distressed us so much. Our self consists of the superimposition of our successive states. But that superimposition, like the stratification on a mountain, is not immutable. Constant upheavals lift ancient strata to the surface. (III, 544–45)*

By way of compensation for the anticipated loss of the wisteria and for the other destruction and upheaval, she planted one *Garrya elliptica* and two *Morella californica* just inside the string stretched along the property line to the west. With the deck gone and built back smaller on that side, the house is more exposed to the neighbors and the village street below, where the two lanes meet at a small bridge over the creek that flows into the bay, really a fjord.

E had been staring death in the face for some time. Her words: I am staring death in the face; this, her visual field. Sometimes she'd say wryly that she wanted it to come faster, that she wanted to wake up dead; others, with even more levity, that she'd like to wake up either dead or able to get out of bed, stand up, walk into the bathroom, stand at the kitchen counter, open the refrigerator, sit at the kitchen table.

If all other entities resounded at once, now and in unison, would their voices finally drown us out?

❖   ❖   ❖

She recalls, with only the prompt of place:

When she was a child, she used to lie in bed in this room, trying to sleep and trying not to feel like a dead person. That's when death hovered and she'd be afraid to close her eyes, death sketched on the insides of her eyelids. Death staring her in the face.

She'd never lie flat on her back in bed with legs outstretched, hands folded over belly or chest. That would be to tempt the fates, summon death closer; because that's how corpses lie in their coffins. That's how it feels to be dead.

Unable to sleep, she would finally get out of bed and open the door and walk quietly into the main room. The book E had been reading would already be on her lap and she would already be looking toward the short hallway where her daughter appeared. This was summer, fog-bound summer with damp and chilly nights.

E might say, You're still awake, and she might answer, I'm having bad thoughts, or, I'm thinking about death.

She also recalls a day soon before E slipped away, sitting in the armchair in E's bedroom, her old bedroom, her bedroom now again, dozing and reading and conversing gently from time to time. E slowly turned her head—in that hush such movements rustle the air—and opened her eyes slightly and asked her if she remembered the conversations they used to have when she couldn't sleep because she was afraid of death.

She said yes, and after a pause E asked if she remembered what she would say to comfort her. She said she didn't.

❖   ❖   ❖

Intervals: that's all there is between this and that, between living and death. Most of us want one more. The intervals between heartbeats, for instance, and those between breaths. The moment she first heard her son's heartbeat: the suggestion of an interval, in this case longer, the last beat farther off, unthinkable but still, an interval revealed through skin and womb.

Shorter or longer intervals. We know how it ends but depending on where we are in the countdown, the difficulty of looking away. To remain in the interval. How can we do that when we are not staring death in the face? For E the intervals consisted of what's for dinner and who will visit and can you read me that poem. Or: another shower an urgent need to pee a morning without morphine another goodbye another visit from another friend another story about the osprey chick in the nest on the Mesa.

She could no longer rise from bed without assistance so had time to mull what should happen when she could no longer wish anything. No memorial of any kind, she told her daughter, I hate memorials. Particularly the ritual of people standing up and speaking about the dead in glowing terms.

Even ash is less bitter. Let there be only ash.

The choice to remain silent. The license to choose to remain silent.

In the same vein, we have tired of constellations. Orion is unavoidable, splayed across the sky, his phallus sword hanging down between his spread-eagle limbs. A crescent moon rising in the east, casting shadows on her nightwalk.

It's now February, and the rain has returned, or promises to. So far, nothing. Only gusts of wind, felt in a draft through the house and in the rustling of bay laurel and live oak branches.

❖　❖　❖

The where is here as never before and likely not for long. While here and now that the journals are stashed, she sits for longer hours and with her attention less divided, reading Proust. Among other subjects, the current volume deals intricately and in great detail with the interactions and relationships among the highest strata of society, the rungs increasingly crowded together, a ladder of the absurd, France in the late nineteenth, early twentieth, century. The hook of rereading might have been her enhanced grasp of threads: to be able to feel at one end the vibrations occurring at the other. Re-verberations. Or: each mention of a particular character stands on a different facet of the crystal in hand, the crystal on which can be seen reflections of the scintillating lights intermittently written.

The intricacies of aristocratic social interactions during the last days of Europe before the First World War, as well as what it's like to not be able to name one's own desire.*

A race weighed down by a curse and forced to live a lie and perjure itself because it knows that its own desire, the source of life's greatest sweetness for all creatures, is deemed punishable and shameful, inadmissible . . . (II, 615)

Throughout the last year of her life, E would mention the cocktail party she looked forward to hosting in death. In life, cocktail parties embodied all she despised about socializing, the trap of the trite and the tediousness of narcissism. Nonetheless, or precisely hence, she derived a previously unknown delight from assembling and disassembling, considering and reconsidering, her own guest list. The stalwarts: Emily Dickinson and Thomas Bernhard and Glenn Gould. Her daughter remembers these in the silence of the house. And silent is what the cocktail party would be with the likes of them, she thinks, Dickinson in a corner practicing her dashes, Bernhard in his wingchair pouting and frowning, Gould running his fingers up and down a keyboard that only he could see or hear. Possibly inspired by Proust's endless social gatherings, hers would bear no resemblance. Socrates had always figured at the top of the guest list, though near the end, a day or two before she died, when the convenient divisions of time and space that order memories and thoughts and habits, that recall contexts, were slipping from her grasp, she blurted out, with no context whatsoever, Socrates's last words, about owing a cock to Asclepius. Her daughter asked her if Socrates was still going to be invited to the cocktail party. E shook her head on the pillow (eyes closed) and said, No. No. Socrates is too harsh.

And so it was that the invitation to the great Greek philosopher was rescinded.

How many times can one thrill at the experience of rain from inside one particular house? Or wind, likewise? Or of being alone in front of the fire? Or the sensation of doubling time, overlaying lives. She sits in this room while the wind howls down the chimney, the rain sheets around her, the house shakes with gusts that peak, then peak again, then continue to blow. The fire is burning low, as has already been described. She reads in Proust a long description of the art of war, the differences in manner and bearing and forms of interaction with other classes between the old aristocracy and that of the Empire, about the narrator's unconvincing passion for Mme de Guermantes, about his sojourn in Doncières with his friend and said Mme's nephew, Robert Saint-Loup, about his maneuverings to get Robert to recommend him to his aunt, and time folds around her as she remembers E sitting in this same room and reading this same book, though in fact she does not remember this, she imagines it, inferring the memory from her knowledge of her having done just that, because she never actually saw her reading Proust in this house. Whenever she arrived, by the time she entered her book would have already been placed on the small wooden end table next to her chair, and she would have looked up, if not gotten up, this depending on the stage of her illness, and by then she would have been the person she knew, not she who she was when she was alone.*

❖ ❖ ❖

* *Alas, that was the phantom I perceived upon entering the drawing room without my grandmother being aware of my return when I found her reading. I was there, or rather, I was not yet there because she didn't know I was there, and . . . she was absorbed in thoughts that she had never revealed in my presence. As for myself—thanks to that fleeting privilege that gives us, for the brief moment of our return, the ability to suddenly be present for our own absence—there was only the witness, the observer, in hat and traveling cloak, the visitor who is not a member of the household, the photographer who comes to take a snapshot of places never to be seen again.* (II, 140)

Birds move too fast, keep too far away for her flawed eyesight to take in fully enough to identify and name. That leaves plants, yes, and mushrooms, given timing and rain. And streets. She's forgotten the names of the streets, or where they lead. So it happens that during the rainstorm she starts the process of reconstructing memory after having decided it is too windy to climb any higher into the forest, after she imagines branches breaking loose and flying through the air or crashing down on her before she could see, let alone decide, where to flee. Instead she wanders through the lanes of the village, all with Scottish names, for the affinities of landscape, the nostalgia of the namers.*

* *Names of things always comply with a notion of the mind, alien to our true impressions, that compels us to eliminate from them everything that does not pertain to that notion.* (I, 835)

But ospreys, yes. The best is to see them flying through the valley. She doesn't actually see them, just their white bellies as they turn, swooping back and forth, only their bellies visible to her against the backdrop of dark green forest from the distance at which she stands at the lookout at the bend of the switchback. They are weaving in and out of the permeable cloth of landscape.

At another moment, shortly before E slipped into her final coma, she turned her head slowly and almost opened her eyes, opened them inside if not opening the lids, and, one by one, without missing anybody, asked if everybody was safe. Her children, her grandchildren, her great nieces and nephews. She checked off the list that had remained intact in her mind to make sure they were not in transit, the phone call had been received that they had arrived home safely, they were, as it were, tucked in, out of danger, the weather, the elements; in harbor. When she reached roughly halfway through the list, she had only to say a name, and her daughter would squeeze her hand and say, yes, she's safe—he's home—she's fine—fine.*

* *The whistle of oxygen would cease for a few seconds. But the happy groan of breathing still gushed forth: light, fitful, unfinished, constantly recommencing. At times it seemed that all was over, the breath had stopped, due perhaps to the changes in octave that occur in a sleeper's respiration, natural intermittence, an effect of the anesthesia, the worsening of her asphyxia, a failure of the heart . . . Who knows if, without my grandmother even being conscious of it, many happy and tender states compressed by her distress were now escaping from her, like those lighter gases so long contained. It was as if everything that she had to tell us was gushing out, that she was addressing that prolixity, that haste, that effusion to us.* (II, 344)

act 3

By now she spends days here in the house and the village and on the trails E loved, through the forest and up to the ridge, without thoughts of E. She hears the wind without imagining her hearing it, and she no longer wonders what E would think of all the changes she has forced the house to undergo. During her walk today, she has a brief intimation of what it might feel like to slip into the place of composition. The bishop pines are swaying and creaking and the forest feels busy, invisibly busy, alive in not just the comforting way that forests *are* alive when you trust they will stay put, but alive in an uncanny way. Then there is the broken branch in the path that suddenly looks like a dead fish, and there are the murmurings from the understory. She quickly leaves that place, for it is an uncomfortable one, and sets about finding the side trail where once she found hedgehog mushrooms and from which the view of the watershed is more inclusive and expansive, then carefully and probably to no avail she pulls up a young fern frond and a huckleberry sprout and a stray salal, which anyway are in the path, anyway will be trampled or deliberately removed, to replant them on the hillside next to the house, a marginally naughty act that she conceals by stuffing their dirty feet under her jacket.*

◈ ◈ ◈

* *But genius, even great talent, comes less from superior aspects of the intellect or from social refinement then from the ability to transform, transpose them. To heat a liquid with an electric lamp one need not have the strongest possible lamp but one in which the current can cease to illuminate, be diverted, and give heat instead of light.* (I, 554)

End of February and spring has arrived without a proper winter. Two bursts of rain then nothing. Despite her feeble fencing efforts the deer nibble heartily on her recently planted *Ceanothus* and even the small *Garrya elliptica*, whose bitter leaves were supposed to deter them.

As soon as she untangles the rope and saws through the makeshift apparatus that never offered proper support to the old gnarled wisteria, the entire twisted sculpted stem collapses. She piles the pieces in an open flat area next to the house, which just recently was cleared. Construction has been at a standstill for more than a month. In the meantime, she continues to plant, now manzanita, now native grasses, and to cut back the beaked hazelnut and the invasive ivy to allow the sun to shine more fully on the grandmother apple tree clinging improbably to the hillside next to the driveway. Her trunk is hollow, yet she flowers and fruits. She should have died years ago. She is older than the house. She is flawless.*

* *In order to understand how beautiful an old woman may once have been, one must not only look at but also translate every feature.* (I, 698)

Awake at three in the morning and into the forest and up to the ridge after reading Proust for several hours. She habitually walks in the afternoons and is now seeing that every day the world is inverted in her absence. As she nears the ridge, she look east, over the bay, and sees a white quiescent sea of fog lying horizontal below her. The three ridges farther east running approximately north-south and almost parallel are like archipelagos, only their peaks high enough to break into an island, or a wave: a frozen wave. The outline of the trees on the ridge to the west is razor sharp against the differently blue sky. Her thoughts, stubborn and disobedient, are churning on everything except the cincture holding in her gaze, the same thoughts that woke her at three and made it impossible for her to lie in bed a single minute longer. The dead might be gone but nobody ever is, and she does not want her churnings to resemble E's churnings, often lamented, sleepless nights often recounted.

She picks up a stick and is able to convince herself, within the confines of reason, that she did so in order to break through the many lines of spider webs stretched across the path, for as lovely as they are especially in the morning light with the dew shimmering and quivering on every fiber, accentuating every juncture, they often hang in shadows, and she had grown tired of wiping the broken threads off her face. But she disbelieves this thin veil of intention, especially on the heels of wanting to break through to some other side and not be she, or E, and in a space blocked off from her other self, she knows that she picked up that stick because she began to ponder the possibility of a mountain lion. Then, without feeling particularly frightened, but holding the stick and waving it in front of her to clear the air of possible spider webs, she imagines the following scenario: Yellow police tape stretched across the narrow fire road that leads into the watershed and this and other paths therein. A sheriff standing guard, others milling around, organizing themselves for a mission. The first local arrives, not aware to what extent he takes for granted his morning walk with his two dogs, a small white one and a golden retriever. He is thoroughly taken aback. What could possibly . . . ? There's been an incident with a mountain lion, says the sheriff, trying to find the right balance between serious warning that would dissuade even the most independent-minded local and unnecessarily gory details. But the local insists and the sheriff is obliged to divulge the fact that there has been an incident that resulted in a fatality. No, we cannot disclose any information about the victim, though the local man, now dissuaded from continuing on his walk, will find out, as will everyone else in the village, that the victim was one K, and that her half-eaten body was found by F of the water department during his daily review of the water collectors. Wasn't she the daughter of E, who used to own the coffee shop, and after that the bookstore? Then she imagines that these thoughts are the last she ever has and wonders if the mountain lion will be able to taste them.*

---

* *But I felt that for her as for the Verdurins, what mattered was not to gaze at the view like tourists, but to partake of good meals, entertain those they liked, write letters, read books, in short, live there, passively allowing its beauty to soak into them rather than making it the object of their attention.* (II, 897–98)

The word *evergreen* belies the nature of springtime in these parts. Green is green but never the same green, the palette is broad, and in spring it expands to twice its size. For each of the multiple greens of the ever variety, there is a new, fresh green, a shade or two lighter, a neighboring hue. It appears at the tips of the branches, painted not to match but to contrast in a lighter shade. The nail tips of the branches form as if a crown over the top of the small grove of oak trees in front of and a little down the hill from the large windows across the front of the house. Already, a month into it, the colors have begun to blend, in sections the crown has evanesced, become dusty, toughened to resist life during the dry half of the year. Deciduous leafings take place on trunks and branches and twigs that have been there all along but astound with their particular shade of green. Hazelnut and buckeye spread their lime-green cloaks through the understory and along edges of drift, edging the forest.

The deck is almost finished. The table saw stands idly in front of the sliding glass doors, like a hooded, tortured prisoner on six legs, the brown tarp tied around its neck with an orange cord, odd pieces of ends scattered about amidst the sawdust. Yes, many nights can pass and mornings be greeted with nothing more than a passing thought of E or death. Or they are no longer thoughts, per se, but rather features on the landscape that we have seen so many times we no longer notice them, like the bare hazelnuts and buckeyes, and that might be what E told her so many years ago, that by the time the time comes, once so many others have gone before, there is indeed an ease, maybe even a tinge of relief.*

❖ ❖ ❖

* *These consecutive deaths, so dreaded by the self that they were going to destroy, so indifferent, so gentle once consummated and when the one who feared them was no longer there to feel them, had long ago made me understand how unwise it would be for me to fear death.* (III, 1038)

Today she walks along the bay, or fjord, at low tide in the late afternoon. Into her mind comes a sentence she has recently read, this one not Proust. *The wind draws its shape upon the water.* Ribbons of glass and patches of ruffled water. Breeze not wind. Also otherwise, the breeze draws upon the water the contours of the land on either side of this narrow bay, under which is a fault, a tectonic boundary, a crack beneath the feet. The land on either side of the bay are moving in opposite directions. She is moving north on the side that is moving north, the forested side.

She walks until she reaches the small cove where she spent long and many summer days as a child. E would drop them off at the trailhead at the top of the hill, and they would walk the half mile or so through the mostly bay laurel forest dripping with moss and bursting with ferns until they reached the first of the two coves, then continue for a short way over the next small ridge, and on the beach in that second cove they would settle for the day. Since the end of childhood, she has longed to return to that cove to swim in that water more often than she has done so. No matter what else seemed to matter at any particular juncture in her life, what conflicts or joys or pains or inaccessible figments she was entertaining, being in that water reconciled her to existence: the sheer joy of having a body that can move through water. Today, in the frigid early spring waters, in addition to large flocks of ducks that suddenly lift off in a flurry, skim the surface, then coast back to a stop, all in perfect synchronization and easy grace, are harbor seals. Some alone, a few in pairs, and one seeming trio, float, dip down then reappear, sometimes following the approximate line the buoys trace in summer and she has traced countless times, stroke after stroke after stroke. One seal lies on her back, her face and belly protruding above the surface of the water. And there, she thinks, float the years and months and weeks and days and hours and minutes that have passed since she was that little girl on that beach, as if it were a physical block of some unknown material in possession of presence but no mass, and not as Proust says. She is saddened by the effort life has been and marvels at how effortless the seal appears to be.*

* *As with the future, it is not all at once but grain by grain that we savor the past.* (III, 531)

A dream. One. She has one dream about the house during her stay. That she learns about a basement room, the size of the house's footprint, though it seems to expand when she enters and begins to explore. She finds it to have three stone fireplaces, each surrounded by sitting areas richly furnished with couches and chairs and rugs and spacious emptiness. The person who leads her down there has known about it for some time, and it is unclear why he has chosen precisely that moment to reveal it to her. She understands that it was kept secret in order to be used as a getaway, a place to be alone, and that through omission she was betrayed by her mother about the nature of this house where she grew up. How could she have never known about this subterranean room, ample and well-appointed?*

* *We can be faithful only to what we remember, and we remember only what we have known.*
(III, 595)

One day, some future day, she will push her hands gently under the mulch and crawl them forward, the palm flat upon the soil, the fingers searching for the crown of the clump whose tops she sees above the rising mound. She knows that it is easier and more effective to take hold of the grass at soil level, and one day, let's say in May, a future May in a year after the drought has passed, a May of late rains after a long winter of consistent, heavy, above-average downpours, an afternoon that portends the coming summer with a high mist that isn't yet fog, in what will by then be a garden, she will consider that gardening, like so much else one does with love, is to a large extent an editorial process, deciding what to leave and what to pull up by the roots.

She doesn't belong here, not anywhere, but if anywhere then here so now where is there to go. She returned to this village months ago to fix up the old family home and find a place for herself amid the plants and the birds and the seashores. Through the forests, onto the hillside across from the house, in the bay so silty. The old apple tree improbably perched on the hillside is flowering profusely from a few hearty branches rising out of a hollow trunk, a canopy is formed, and the apples will be, by early August, as sweet as when she first tasted them as a little girl. She, the tree, belongs, and thereby, let us define belonging.

She has learned the names of some of the plants, tried with birds but failed, let's say because of her eyesight, hoped for mushrooms but then the drought, and is determined still, next time, to learn the names of the shorebirds. It started there, then, at the beach last November, when she thought that one mostly doesn't have the courage to listen to the surf, crimson crashing with those insistent whispers, or wonder at the mauve foam, the afterbirth of waves, or stay once the sanderlings have gone.*

* *We dream often about paradise, or rather about many successive paradises, but long before we die they are all paradises lost, and where we would feel lost.* (II, 859)

What might she have expected? True to her species, she came with plans to master the world, in her case, for example, by learning the names of other species. For example, by reading a geological history of the area. For example, by exploring village life, through its craftspeople, its merchants, its assorted locals and visitors. But not once, till now, has she simply sat and watched, lived outside, anywhere, with the other creatures. Two blue jays, young ones, teenagers, as E used to call them with reluctant and derisive affection, are sitting just to the side over the deck on the electric wire that stretches from the pole at the top of the driveway to the roof. They came groomed and are now ruffling their own feathers, a ritual of repulsion or attraction. They fly off and now a crow arrives and sits alone, though his or her mate must be nearby. They caw incessantly and are said to flourish at the expense of songbirds. She watches another crow fly past the second row of trees.

She has overstayed her welcome. We all have. Today, at the ocean beach, all the people were feeding and very well fed, even obese, and a starving seal pup struggled to get back to the sea faster than the retreating tide.*

* *Surely names are fanciful draftsmen, giving us sketches of people and places so inaccurate that we experience a kind of astonishment when we have before us, instead of the imagined world, the visible world (still not the real world, our senses hardly possess more talent for accuracy than our imagination, such that the ultimately approximate drafts one can obtain of reality are at least as different from the seen world than those were from the imagined world) . . .* (I, 548)

It is impossible to write and observe at the same time. It is impossible to observe and render thought into words, collections of words, syntactic structures composed of words, at the same time. Hence, a tripartite process. A sleight of hand: the illusion of simultaneity.

The act of writing, then, as a contrived rendition of the act of perception. Poetry returning us with a better or worse sense of direction to perception itself, as if magically transported three steps in each direction into the serenity of the moment. Sleight of hand.

In this house with the view of the facing forest a simulacrum of which has been forever the backdrop of her life, always there even if often obscured by present tenses, she muses on the triumph of being able to spend long stretches of time without thinking of E or, now, her journals, of sleeping soundly and without thoughts of death as a monster fast approaching, instead fleetingly as a goal that will be achieved at a date unknown. Tonight, here, in the fading evening light when the sky is that color between gray and blue and white, when the light is so low that the sky anyway is bleached, she is no longer younger than E; she is no longer her survivor who must somehow deny her even if it is by affirming everything she was; she is no longer here to claim this house this view this particular angle on the world, a green benevolent world, just wild enough, of few if any threats of violence or brutality, for herself, to wrestle this possibility away from her. She no longer does this. Instead, they sit together and share the view.*

❖ ❖ ❖

* An hour is not only an hour, it is a vase filled with scents, sounds, plans, and atmospheres. What we call reality is the specific relationship between the sensations and the memories that surround us simultaneously . . . a unique relationship that the writer must recover in order to shackle the two different terms together forever in her sentence . . . truth will only begin at the moment the writer takes two different objects, presents their relationship . . . (III, 889)

She is far richer now for having sat on the same side as E and with her looked out onto the hillside facing the house in the fading light, before the color of the light makes it impossible to know if there is fog or clear skies, and for a moment sense an overlapping. They are, no longer, vying. Now she can begin to wonder in earnest how E might have felt on some odd day that was never recorded by any device whatsoever but that had to have happened, in May, say, the day before her daughter's birthday, which would always for her as well as for her be the day before her daughter's birthday, how she must have felt as she sat on her deck and watched a deer saunter up the driveway—sniffing here and then there, looking for choice morsels of new-grown green—and admired her impossible grace and cursed her appetite, sitting quietly so as not to shake the deer's purpose, so as to discover her patterns of grazing; how she must have felt as she watched the ridgeline dim, wisps of fog brushing in front of the longest highest arms of the bishop pines; how she must have felt and what words she would have used to articulate only to herself that experience.

This, she's never stopped and watched before. This onrush of fog from the west. From the ocean beyond the ridge. In the fading evening light. Against the darkening line of trees along the ridge. The dome above illuminated from below. Gray now, the sun having descended or (this imagined) hidden behind more stubborn clouds. There is as if a funnel from the coast. Light travels with the clouds, higher up, reflecting.*

* *Thus I had already reached the conclusion that we are not at all free regarding a work of art, that we do not create it according to our will, but that, preexisting us, because it is both necessary and concealed, and as we would in obedience to a law of nature, we must discover it. But this discovery that art could have us make, wasn't it, deep down, what should be most precious to us, and what usually remains forever unknown, our true life, reality such as we have felt it and that so greatly differs from what we believe, such that we are filled with great joy when by chance it brings us genuine remembering?* (III, 881)

She sleeps so well in the room that was her bedroom as a child and that was her mother's bedroom and her mother's deathroom that when she wakes she suspects that she has been elsewhere but no memory remains. When she gets into bed she is enveloped in a shroud of soft leanings, one that is just tight enough to comfort but not suffocate. Not unlike though wholly different from diving into the bay, though in that case the shroud is icy and mercurial, sweeping gracefully and in full measure around her entire body and moving in perfect harmony as she catches her breath stolen in that initial wild rush, the movements of her limbs at first like panting, a quickening of all systems until a precariously stable state is reached. It is, of course, no more so than any other state, though it is not the duration of suspension of perceptible change so much as a synching however briefly of the intrinsic and the extrinsic, when the breath, for instance, can luxuriate in its filling as in its emptying, when the arc of the arm is not compromised by that slight crook in the elbow that presses into a lengthening of the body, fingertip to toe, as the body turns, as the body comes to rest.*

❖   ❖   ❖

* *All of a sudden I'd fall asleep, plunge into that deep slumber wherein is revealed to us the return to childhood, the recovery of years past, of lost feelings, of disembodiment, the transmigration of souls, the evocation of the dead, the illusions of madness, the relapse to the most elementary realms of nature . . . all those mysteries we believe we don't know when, in fact, we are initiated into them almost every night, as well as into the other great mystery of death and resurrection. (I, 819–20)*

Even though I may return, even for long stretches, this stretch has concluded and the combination of relief and grief is baffling. For the first time since I began to write these notes, each at a single sitting, never more than one sitting per day, I am not there, now, at this moment. On my way there I didn't know I was going to look for her, for them, and I didn't, not really, that anyway being a metaphor and I preferring to look for another.

I've left the journals behind and stashed away, be that as it may. I've also left the two of them behind, sitting on the deck, noticing the crow on the wire and the bishop pines that form the line of treetops along the facing ridge, the ones reaching out with flailing limbs, stretching impossibly toward the sky that lowers its fog to them. I've left them behind sitting and watching the fire while the wind howls and the rain shutters down tumbling across the roof. I've left them behind curled up blissfully in that whistling cold bedroom, in the warm bed under layers of down bedding, fully confident that once rest is assumed, the body accommodated to the contour of the old mattress and the pillows properly arranged, sleep will come and be delicious in the way that it negates all we know or thought we knew a moment before and replaced it with something we never would know fully. I've left them behind wrestling with the blackberry, tearing out the ivy, clearing the driveway, spreading the oak mulch, noticing the reach of the oak trees and knowing that however sweeping their gesture, it would have to one day be cut short. I've left them at peace with all the lovers they've ever had, without a drop of shame about one kind over another, wholly at peace with all the love they've been able to give and receive rather than just the pain of losing, of being lost, of losing. I've left them behind having chosen to be alone so they can each hear herself think. I've left them behind with the song from the bird neither ever managed to see but that sang so sweetly it made their hearts wince at the paucity of real beauty they managed to behold. What might a memory be? And, what does it mean to remember oneself?

And I've left them sitting in a chair in the front room, their backs to the forested mountain across the small valley, reading Proust, or something, anything, else, for hours at a time. That's where I'll find them when I return.

WHAT
BOOKS
PRESS

LOS ANGELES

OTHER TITLES FROM WHAT BOOKS PRESS

ART

Gronk, A Giant Claw
Bilingual, spanish

Chuck Rosenthal, Gail Wronsky & Gronk,
Tomorrow You'll Be One of Us: Sci Fi Poems

PROSE

François Camoin, *April, May, and So On*

A.W. DeAnnuntis, *The Mysterious Islands and Other Stories*

Katharine Haake, *The Time of Quarantine*

Mona Houghton, *Frottage & Even As We Speak: Two Novellas*

Rod Val Moore, *Brittle Star*

Chuck Rosenthal, *Coyote O'Donohughe's History of Texas*

NON-FICTION

Chuck Rosenthal, *West of Eden: A Life in 21st Century Los Angeles*

POETRY

Kevin Cantwell, *One of Those Russian Novels*

Ramón García, *Other Countries*

Karen Kevorkian, *Lizard Dream*

Gail Wronsky, *Imperfect Pastorals*

WHATBOOKSPRESS.COM

CPSIA information can be obtained
at www.ICGtesting.com
Printed in the USA
FSHW011259231219
65393FS